The Snow Queen

A TALE IN SEVEN STORIES

HANS CHRISTIAN ANDERSEN

Illustrated by
SANNA ANNUKKA

Translated by
JEAN HERSHOLT

TEN SPEED PRESS
Berkeley

Illustrations copyright © 2015 by Sanna Annukka
Translation copyright © 2015 Odense City Museums

Originally published in Great Britain by Hutchinson,
a Penguin Random House Company, London, in 2015.

Library of Congress Cataloging-in-Publication Data
is on file with the publisher

Hardcover ISBN: 978-0-399-57850-2
eBook ISBN: 978-0-399-57851-9

Printed in China

Typeset by Lindsay Nash

10 9 8 7 6 5 4 3 2 1

First American Edition, 2016

FOR
KASPER & ELKA

FIRST STORY

WHICH HAS TO DO WITH A MIRROR AND ITS FRAGMENTS

Now then! We will begin. When the story is done you shall know a great deal more than you do now.

He was a terribly bad hobgoblin, a goblin of the very wickedest sort and, in fact, he was the devil himself. One day the devil was in a very good humour because he had just finished a mirror which had this peculiar power: everything good and beautiful that was reflected in it seemed to dwindle to almost nothing at all, while everything that was worthless and ugly became most conspicuous and even uglier than ever. In this mirror the loveliest landscapes looked like boiled spinach, and the very best people became hideous, or stood on their heads and had no stomachs. Their faces were distorted beyond any recognition, and if a person had a freckle it was sure to spread until it covered both nose and mouth.

'That's very funny!' said the devil. If a good, pious thought passed through anyone's mind, it showed in the mirror as a carnal grin, and the devil laughed aloud at his ingenious invention.

All those who went to the hobgoblin's school – for he had a school of his own – told everyone that a miracle had come to pass. Now, they asserted, for the very first time you could see how the world and its people really looked. They scurried about with the mirror until there was not a person alive nor a land on earth that had not been distorted.

hen they wanted to fly up to heaven itself, to scoff at the angels, and our Lord. The higher they flew with the mirror, the wider it grinned. They could hardly manage to hold it. Higher they flew, and higher still, nearer to heaven and the angels. Then the grinning mirror trembled with such violence that it slipped from their hands and fell to the earth, where it shattered into hundreds of millions of billions of bits, or perhaps even more. And now it caused more trouble than it did before it was broken, because some of the fragments were smaller than a grain of sand and these went flying throughout the wide world. Once they got in people's eyes they would stay there. These bits of glass distorted everything the people saw, and made them see only the bad side of things, for every little bit of glass kept the same power that the whole mirror had possessed.

A few people even got a glass splinter in their hearts, and that was a terrible thing, for it turned their hearts into lumps of ice. Some fragments were so large that they were used as window panes – but not the kind of window through which you should look at your friends. Other pieces were made into spectacles, and evil things came to pass when people put them on to see clearly and to see justice done. The fiend was so tickled by it all that he laughed till his sides were sore. But fine bits of the glass are still flying through the air, and now you shall hear what happened.

SECOND STORY

A LITTLE BOY AND A LITTLE GIRL

In the big city it was so crowded with houses and people that few found room for even a small garden and most people had to be content with a flowerpot, but two poor children who lived there managed to have a garden that was a little bigger than a flowerpot. These children were not brother and sister, but they loved each other just as much as if they had been. Their parents lived close to one another in the garrets of two adjoining houses. Where the roofs met and where the rain gutter ran between the two houses, their two small windows faced each other. One had only to step across the rain gutter to go from window to window.

In these windows, the parents had a large box where they planted vegetables for their use, and a little rose bush too. Each box had a bush, which thrived to perfection. Then it occurred to the parents to put these boxes across the gutter, where they very nearly reached from one window to the other, and looked exactly like two walls of flowers. The pea plants hung down over the boxes, and the rose bushes threw out long sprays that framed the windows and bent over towards each other. It was almost like a little triumphal arch of greenery and flowers.

he boxes were very high, and the children knew that they were not to climb about on them, but they were often allowed to take their little stools out on the roof under the roses, where they had a wonderful time playing together.

Winter, of course, put an end to this pleasure. The windows often frosted over completely. But they would heat copper pennies on the stove and press these hot coins against the frost-coated glass. Then they had the finest of peepholes, as round as a ring, and behind them appeared a bright, friendly eye, one at each window – it was the little boy and the little girl who peeped out. His name was Kay and hers was Gerda. With one skip they could join each other in summer, but to visit together in the wintertime they had to go all the way downstairs in one house, and climb all the way upstairs in the other. Outside the snow was whirling.

'See the white bees swarming,' the old grand-mother said.

'Do they have a queen bee, too?' the little boy asked, for he knew that real bees have one.

'Yes, indeed they do,' the grandmother said. 'She flies in the thick of the swarm. She is the biggest bee of all, and can never stay quietly on the earth, but goes back again to the dark clouds. Many a wintry night she flies through the streets and peers in through the windows. Then they freeze over in a strange fashion, as if they were covered with flowers.'

'Oh yes, we've seen that,' both the children said, and so they knew it was true.

'Can the Snow Queen come in here?' the little girl asked.

'Well, let her come!' cried the boy. 'I would put her on the hot stove and melt her.'

But Grandmother stroked his head, and told them other stories.

That evening when little Kay was at home and half ready for bed, he climbed on the chair by the window and looked out through the little peephole. A few snowflakes were falling, and the largest flake of all alighted on the edge of one of the flower boxes. This flake grew bigger and bigger, until at last it turned into a woman, who was dressed in the finest white gauze, which looked as if it had been made from millions of star-shaped flakes. She was beautiful and she was graceful, but she was ice —shining, glittering ice. She was alive, for all that, and her eyes sparkled like two bright stars, but in them there was neither rest nor peace.

he nodded towards the window and beckoned with her hand. The little boy was frightened, and as he jumped down from the chair it seemed to him that a huge bird flew past the window.

The next day was clear and cold. Then the snow thawed, and springtime came. The sun shone, the green grass sprouted, swallows made their nests, windows were thrown open, and once again the children played in their little roof garden, high up in the rain gutter on top of the house.

That summer the roses bloomed their splendid best. The little girl had learned a hymn in which there was a line about roses that reminded her of their own flowers. She sang it to the little boy, and he sang it with her:

> *'Where roses bloom so sweetly in the vale,*
> *There shall you find the Christ Child, without fail.'*

The children held each other by the hand, kissed the roses, looked up at the Lord's clear sunshine, and spoke to it as if the Christ Child were there. What glorious summer days those were, and how beautiful it was out under those fragrant rose bushes which seemed as if they would never stop blooming.

ay and Gerda were looking at a picture book of birds and beasts one day, and it was then — just as the clock in the church tower was striking five — that Kay cried:

'Oh! something hurt my heart. And now I've got something in my eye.'

The little girl put her arm around his neck, and he blinked his eye. No, she couldn't see anything in it.

'I think it's gone,' he said. But it was not gone. It was one of those splinters of glass from the magic mirror. You remember that goblin's mirror – the one which made everything great and good that was reflected in it appear small and ugly, but which magnified all evil things until each blemish loomed large. Poor Kay! A fragment had pierced his heart as well, and soon it would turn into a lump of ice. The pain had stopped, but the glass was still there.

'Why should you be crying?' he asked. 'It makes you look so ugly. There's nothing the matter with me.' And suddenly he took it into his head to say:

'Ugh! That rose is all worm-eaten. And look, this one is crooked. And these roses, they are just as ugly as they can be. They look like the boxes they grow in.' He gave the boxes a kick, and broke off both of the roses.

'Kay! What are you doing?' the little girl cried. When he saw how it upset her, he broke off another rose and then leaped home through his own window, leaving dear little Gerda all alone.

Afterwards, when she brought out her picture book, he said it was fit only for babes in the cradle. And whenever Grandmother told stories, he always broke in with a 'but –.' If he could manage it he would steal behind her, perch a pair of spectacles on his nose, and imitate her. He did this so cleverly that it made everybody laugh, and before long he could mimic the walk and the talk of everyone who lived on that street. Everything that was odd or ugly about them, Kay could mimic so well that people said, 'That boy has surely got a good head on him!' But it was the glass in his eye and the glass in his heart that made him tease even little Gerda, who loved him with all her soul.

ow his games were very different from what they used to be. They became more sensible. When the snow was flying about one wintry day, he brought a large magnifying glass out of doors and spread the tail of his blue coat to let the snowflakes fall on it.

'Now look through the glass,' he told Gerda. Each snowflake seemed much larger, and looked like a magnificent flower or a ten-pointed star. It was marvellous to look at.

'Look, how artistic!' said Kay. 'They are much more interesting to look at than real flowers, for they are absolutely perfect. There isn't a flaw in them, until they start melting.'

A little while later Kay came down with his big gloves on his hands and his sled on his back. Right in Gerda's ear he bawled out, 'I've been given permission to play in the big square where the other boys are!' and away he ran.

In the square some of the more adventuresome boys would tie their little sleds on behind the farmers' carts, to be pulled along for quite a distance. It was wonderful sport. While the fun was at its height, a big sleigh drove up. It was painted entirely white, and the driver wore a white, shaggy fur cloak and a white, shaggy cap.

As the sleigh drove twice around the square, Kay quickly hooked his little sled behind it, and down the street they went, faster and faster. The driver turned around in a friendly fashion and nodded to Kay, just as if they were old acquaintances. Every time Kay started to unfasten his little sleigh, its driver nodded again, and Kay held on, even when they drove right out through the town gate.

Then the snow began to fall so fast that the boy could not see his hands in front of him, as they sped on. He suddenly let go the slack of the rope in his hands, in order to get loose from the big sleigh, but it did no good. His little sled was tied on securely, and they went like the wind. He gave a loud shout, but nobody heard him. The snow whirled and the sleigh flew along. Every now and then it gave a jump, as if it were clearing hedges and ditches. The boy was terror-stricken. He tried to say his prayers, but all he could remember was his multiplication tables.

The snowflakes got bigger and bigger, until they looked like big white hens. All of a sudden the curtain of snow parted, and the big sleigh stopped and the driver stood up. The fur coat and the cap were made of snow, and it was a woman, tall and slender and blinding white – she was the Snow Queen herself.

'We have made good time,' she said. 'Is it possible that you tremble from cold? Crawl under my bear coat.' She took him up in the sleigh beside her, and as she wrapped the fur about him he felt as if he were sinking into a snowdrift.

'Are you still cold?' she asked, and kissed him on the forehead. *Brr-r-r*. That kiss was colder than ice. He felt it right down to his heart, half of which was already an icy lump. He felt as if he were dying, but only for a moment. Then he felt quite comfortable, and no longer noticed the cold.

'My sled! Don't forget my sled!' It was the only thing he thought of. They tied it to one of the white hens, which flew along after them with the sled on its back. The Snow Queen kissed Kay once more, and then he forgot little Gerda, and Grandmother, and all the others at home.

'ou won't get any more kisses now,' she said, 'or else I should kiss you to death.' Kay looked at her. She was so beautiful! A cleverer and prettier face he could not imagine. She no longer seemed to be made of ice, as she had seemed when she sat outside his window and beckoned to him. In his eyes she was perfect, and he was not at all afraid. He told her how he could do mental arithmetic even with fractions, and that he knew the size and population of all the countries. She kept on smiling, and he began to be afraid that he did not know as much as he thought he did. He looked up at the great big space overhead, as she flew with him high up on the black clouds, while the storm whistled and roared as if it were singing old ballads.

They flew over forests and lakes, over many a land and sea. Below them the wind blew cold, wolves howled, and black crows screamed as they skimmed across the glittering snow. But up above the moon shone bright and large, and on it Kay fixed his eyes throughout that long, long winter night. By day he slept at the feet of the Snow Queen.

THIRD STORY

THE FLOWER GARDEN OF THE WOMAN SKILLED IN MAGIC

How did little Gerda get along when Kay did not come back? Where could he be? Nobody knew. Nobody could give them any news of him. All that the boys could say was that they had seen him hitch his little sled to a fine big sleigh, which had driven down the street and out through the town gate. Nobody knew what had become of Kay. Many tears were shed, and little Gerda sobbed hardest of all. People said that he was dead – that he must have been drowned in the river not far from town. Ah, how gloomy those long winter days were!

But spring and its warm sunshine came at last.

'Kay is dead and gone,' little Gerda said.

'I don't believe it,' said the sunshine.

'He's dead and gone,' she said to the swallows.

'We don't believe it,' they sang. Finally little Gerda began to disbelieve it too. One morning she said to herself: 'I'll put on my new red shoes, the ones Kay has never seen, and I'll go down by the river to ask about him.'

It was very early in the morning. She kissed her old grandmother, who was still asleep, put on her red shoes, and all by herself she hurried out through the town gate and down to the river.

'Is it true that you have taken my own little playmate? I'll give you my red shoes if you will bring him back to me.'

It seemed to her that the waves nodded very strangely. So she took off her red shoes that were her dearest possession, and threw them into the river. But they fell near the shore, and the little waves washed them right back to her. It seemed that the river could not take her dearest possession, because it did not have little Kay. However, she was afraid that she had not thrown them far enough, so she clambered into a boat that lay among the reeds, walked to the end of it, and threw her shoes out into the water again. But the boat was not tied, and her movements made it drift away from the bank. She realised this, and tried to get ashore, but by the time she reached the other end of the boat it was already more than a yard from the bank, and was fast gaining speed.

Little Gerda was so frightened that she began to cry, and no one was there to hear her except the sparrows. They could not carry her to land, but they flew along the shore twittering, 'We are here! Here we are!' as if to comfort her.

he boat drifted swiftly down the stream, and Gerda sat there quite still, in her stockinged feet. Her little red shoes floated along behind, but they could not catch up with her because the boat was gathering speed. It was very pretty on both sides of the river, where the flowers were lovely, the trees were old, and the hillsides afforded pasture for cattle and sheep. But not one single person did Gerda see.

'Perhaps the river will take me to little Kay,' she thought, and that made her feel more cheerful. She stood up and watched the lovely green banks for hour after hour.

Then she came to a large cherry orchard, in which there was a little house with strange red and blue windows. It had a thatched roof, and outside it stood two wooden soldiers, who presented arms to everyone who sailed past.

Gerda thought they were alive, and called out to them, but of course they did not answer her. She drifted quite close to them as the current drove the boat towards the bank. Gerda called even louder, and an old, old woman came out of the house. She leaned on a crooked stick; she had on a big sun hat, and on it were painted the most glorious flowers.

'You poor little child!' the old woman exclaimed. 'However did you get lost on this big swift river, and however did you drift so far into the great wide world?'

The old woman waded right into the water, caught hold of the boat with her crooked stick, pulled it in to shore, and lifted little Gerda out of it.

Gerda was very glad to be on dry land again, but she felt a little afraid of this strange old woman, who said to her:

'Come and tell me who you are, and how you got here.' Gerda told her all about it. The woman shook her head and said, 'Hmm, hmm!' And when Gerda had told her everything and asked if she hadn't seen little Kay, the woman said he had not yet come by, but that he might be along any day now. And she told Gerda not to take it so to heart, but to taste her cherries and to look at her flowers. These were more beautiful than any picture book, and each one had a story to tell. Then she led Gerda by the hand into her little house, and the old woman locked the door.

The windows were placed high up on the walls, and through their red, blue, and yellow panes the sunlight streamed in a strange mixture of all the colours there are. But on the table were the most delicious cherries, and Gerda, who was no longer afraid, ate as many as she liked. While she was eating them, the old woman combed her hair with a golden comb. Gerda's pretty hair fell in shining yellow ringlets on either side of a friendly little face that was as round and blooming as a rose.

'I've so often wished for a dear little girl like you,' the old woman told her. 'Now you'll see how well the two of us will get along.'

hile her hair was being combed, Gerda gradually forgot all about Kay, for the old woman was skilled in magic. But she was not a wicked witch. She only dabbled in magic to amuse herself, but she wanted very much to keep little Gerda. So she went out into her garden and pointed her crooked stick at all the rose bushes. In the full bloom of their beauty, all of them sank down into the black earth, without leaving a single trace behind. The old woman was afraid that if Gerda saw them they would remind her so strongly of her own roses, and of little Kay, that she would run away again.

Then Gerda was led into the flower garden. How fragrant and lovely it was! Every known flower of every season was there in full bloom. No picture book was ever so pretty and gay. Gerda jumped for joy, and played in the garden until the sun went down behind the tall cherry trees. Then she was tucked into a beautiful bed, under a red silk coverlet quilted with blue violets. There she slept, and there she dreamed as gloriously as any queen would on her wedding day.

The next morning she again went out into the warm sunshine to play with the flowers – and this she did for many a day. Gerda knew every flower by heart, and, plentiful though they were, she always felt that there was one missing, but which one she didn't quite know.

ne day she sat looking at the old woman's sun hat, and the prettiest of all the flowers painted on it was a rose. The old woman had forgotten this rose on her hat when she made the real roses disappear into the earth. But that's just the sort of thing that happens when one doesn't stop to think.

'Why aren't there any roses here?' said Gerda. She rushed out among the flower beds, and she looked and she looked, but there wasn't a rose to be seen. Then she sat down and cried. But her hot tears fell on the very spot where a rose bush had sunk into the ground, and when her warm tears moistened the earth the bush sprang up again, as full of blossoms as when it disappeared. Gerda hugged it, and kissed the roses. She remembered her own pretty roses, and thought of little Kay.

'Oh, how long I have been delayed,' the little girl said. 'I should have been looking for Kay. Don't you know where he is?' she asked the roses. 'Do you think that he is dead and gone?'

'He isn't dead,' the roses told her. 'We have been down in the earth where the dead people are, but Kay is not there.'

'Thank you,' said little Gerda, who went to all the other flowers, put her lips near them and asked, 'Do you know where little Kay is?'

But every flower stood in the sun, and dreamed its own fairy tale, or its story. Though Gerda listened to many, many of them, not one of the flowers knew anything about Kay.

What did the tiger lily say?

'Do you hear the drum? *Boom, boom!* It was only two notes, always *boom, boom!* Hear the women wail. Hear the priests chant. The Hindu woman in her long red robe stands on the funeral pyre. The flames rise around her and her dead husband, but the Hindu woman is thinking of that living man in the crowd around them. She is thinking of him whose eyes are burning hotter than the flames – of him whose fiery glances have pierced her heart more deeply than these flames that soon will burn her body to ashes. Can the flame of the heart die in the flame of the funeral pyre?'

'I don't understand that at all,' little Gerda said.

'That's my fairy tale,' said the lily.

What did the trumpet flower say?

'An ancient castle rises high from a narrow path in the mountains. The thick ivy grows leaf upon leaf where it climbs to the balcony. There stands a beautiful maiden.

'She leans out over the balustrade to look down the path. No rose on its stem is as graceful as she, nor is any apple blossom in the breeze so light. Hear the rustle of her silk gown, sighing, "Will he never come?"'

'Do you mean Kay?' little Gerda asked.

'I am talking about my story, my own dream,' the trumpet flower replied.

What did the little snowdrop say?

'Between the trees a board hangs by two ropes. It is a swing. Two pretty little girls, with frocks as white as snow, and long green ribbons fluttering from their hats, are swinging. Their brother, who is bigger than they are, stands behind them on the swing, with his arms around the ropes to hold himself. In one hand he has a little cup, and in the other a clay pipe. He is blowing soap bubbles, and as the swing flies the bubbles float off in all their changing colours. The last bubble is still clinging to the bowl of his pipe, and fluttering in the air as the swing sweeps to and fro. A little black dog, light as a bubble, is standing on his hind legs and trying to get up in the swing. But it does not stop. High and low the swing flies, until the dog loses his balance, barks, and loses his temper. They tease him, and the bubble bursts. A swinging board pictured in a bubble before it broke – that is my story.'

‘It may be a very pretty story, but you told it very sadly and you didn't mention Kay at all.'

What did the hyacinths say?

'There were three sisters, quite transparent and very fair. One wore a red dress, the second wore a blue one, and the third went all in white. Hand in hand they danced in the clear moonlight, beside a calm lake. They were not elfin folk. They were human beings. The air was sweet, and the sisters disappeared into the forest. The fragrance of the air grew sweeter. Three coffins, in which lie the three sisters, glide out of the forest and across the lake. The fireflies hover about them like little flickering lights. Are the dancing sisters sleeping or are they dead? The fragrance of the flowers says they are dead, and the evening bell tolls for their funeral.'

'You are making me very unhappy,' little Gerda said. 'Your fragrance is so strong that I cannot help thinking of those dead sisters.

'h, could little Kay really be dead? The roses have been down under the ground, and they say no.'

'Ding, dong,' tolled the hyacinth bells. 'We do not toll for little Kay. We do not know him. We are simply singing our song – the only song we know.'

And Gerda went on to the buttercup that shone among its glossy green leaves.

'You are like a bright little sun,' said Gerda. 'Tell me, do you know where I can find my playmate?'

And the buttercup shone brightly as it looked up at Gerda. But what sort of song would a buttercup sing? It certainly wouldn't be about Kay.

'In a small courtyard, God's sun was shining brightly on the very first day of spring. Its beams glanced along the white wall of the house next door, and close by grew the first yellow flowers of spring shining like gold in the warm sunlight. An old grandmother was sitting outside in her chair. Her granddaughter, a poor but very pretty maidservant, had just come home for a little visit. She kissed her grandmother, and there was gold, a heart full of gold, in that kiss. Gold on her lips, gold in her dreams, and gold above in the morning beams. There, I've told you my little story,' said the buttercup.

'y poor old grandmother,' said Gerda. 'She will miss me so. She must be grieving for me as much as she did for little Kay. But I'll soon go home again, and I'll bring Kay with me. There's no use asking the flowers about him. They don't know anything except their own songs, and they haven't any news for me.'

Then she tucked up her little skirts so that she could run away faster, but the narcissus tapped against her leg as she was jumping over it. So she stopped and leaned over the tall flower.

'Perhaps you have something to tell me,' she said.

What did the narcissus say?

'I can see myself! I can see myself! Oh, how sweet is my own fragrance! Up in the narrow garret there is a little dancer, half dressed. First she stands on one leg. Then she stands on both, and kicks her heels at the whole world. She is an illusion of the stage. She pours water from the teapot over a piece of cloth she is holding – it is her bodice. Cleanliness is such a virtue! Her white dress hangs from a hook. It too has been washed in the teapot, and dried on the roof. She puts it on, and ties a saffron scarf around her neck to make the dress seem whiter. Point your toes! See how straight she balances on that single stem. I can see myself! I can see myself!'

'I'm not interested,' said Gerda. 'What a thing to tell me about!'

She ran to the end of the garden, and though the gate was fastened she worked the rusty latch till it gave way and the gate flew open. Little Gerda scampered out into the wide world in her bare feet. She looked back three times, but nobody came after her. At last she could run no farther, and she sat down to rest on a big stone, and when she looked up she saw that summer had gone by, and it was late in the autumn. She could never have guessed it inside the beautiful garden where the sun was always shining, and the flowers of every season were always in full bloom.

'Gracious! How long I've dallied,' Gerda said. 'Autumn is already here. I can't rest any longer.'

She got up to run on, but how footsore and tired she was! And how cold and bleak everything around her looked! The long leaves of the willow tree had turned quite yellow, and damp puffs of mist dropped from them like drops of water. One leaf after another fell to the ground. Only the blackthorn still bore fruit, and its fruit was so sour that it set your teeth on edge.

Oh, how dreary and grey the wide world looked.

FOURTH STORY
THE PRINCE AND THE PRINCESS

The next time that Gerda was forced to rest, a big crow came hopping across the snow in front of her. For a long time he had been watching her and cocking his head to one side, and now he said, 'Caw, caw! Good caw day!' He could not say it any better, but he felt kindly inclined towards the little girl, and asked her where she was going in the great wide world, all alone. Gerda understood him when he said 'alone,' and she knew its meaning all too well. She told the crow the whole story of her life, and asked if he hadn't seen Kay. The crow gravely nodded his head and cawed, 'Maybe I have, maybe I have!'

'What! Do you really think you have?' the little girl cried, and almost hugged the crow to death as she kissed him.

'Gently, gently!' said the crow. 'I think that it may have been little Kay that I saw, but if it was, then he has forgotten you for the Princess.'

'Does he live with a princess?' Gerda asked.

'Yes. Listen!' said the crow. 'But it is so hard for me to speak your language. If you understand crow talk, I can tell you much more easily.'

'I don't know that language,' said Gerda. 'My grandmother knows it, just as well as she knows baby talk, and I do wish I had learned it.'

'No matter,' said the crow. 'I'll tell you as well as I can, though that won't be any too good.' And he told her all that he knew.

'In the kingdom where we are now, there is a princess who is uncommonly clever, and no wonder. She has read all the newspapers in the world and forgotten them again – that's how clever she is. Well, not long ago she was sitting on her throne. That's by no means as much fun as people suppose, so she fell to humming an old tune, and the refrain of it happened to run:

'"*Why, oh, why, shouldn't I get married?*"

'"Why, that's an idea!" said she. And she made up her mind to marry as soon as she could find the sort of husband who could give a good answer when anyone spoke to him, instead of one of those fellows who merely stand around looking impressive, for that is so tiresome. She had the drums drubbed to call together all her ladies-in-waiting, and when they heard what she had in mind they were delighted.

'"Oh, we like that!" they said. "We were just thinking the very same thing."

'Believe me,' said the crow, 'every word I tell you is true. I have a tame ladylove who has the run of the palace, and I had the whole story straight from her.' Of course his ladylove was also a crow, for birds of a feather will flock together.

'The newspapers immediately came out with a border of hearts and the initials of the Princess, and you could read an announcement that any presentable young man might go to the palace and talk with her. The one who spoke best, and who seemed most at home in the palace, would be chosen by the Princess as her husband.

'Yes, yes,' said the crow, 'believe me, that's as true as it is that here I sit. Men flocked to the palace, and there was much crowding and crushing, but on neither the first nor the second day was anyone chosen. Out in the street they were all glib talkers, but after they entered the palace gate where the guardsmen were stationed in their silver-braided uniforms, and after they climbed up the staircase lined with footmen in gold-embroidered livery, they arrived in the brilliantly lighted reception halls without a word to say. And when they stood in front of the Princess on her throne, the best they could do was to echo the last word of her remarks, and she didn't care to hear it repeated.

'It was just as if everyone in the throne room had his stomach filled with snuff and had fallen asleep; for as soon as they were back in the streets there was no stopping their talk.

'The line of candidates extended all the way from the town gates to the palace. I saw them myself,' said the crow. 'They got hungry and they got thirsty, but from the palace they got nothing – not even a glass of lukewarm water. To be sure, some of the clever candidates had brought sandwiches with them, but they did not share them with their neighbours. Each man thought, "Just let him look hungry, then the Princess won't take him!"'

'ut Kay, little Kay,' Gerda interrupted, 'when did he come? Was he among those people?'

'Give me time, give me time! We are just coming to him. On the third day a little person, with neither horse nor carriage, strode boldly up to the palace. His eyes sparkled the way yours do, and he had handsome long hair, but his clothes were poor.'

'Oh, that was Kay!' Gerda said, and clapped her hands in glee. 'Now I've found him.'

'He had a little knapsack on his back,' the crow told her.

'No, that must have been his sled,' said Gerda. 'He was carrying it when he went away.'

'Maybe so,' the crow said. 'I didn't look at it carefully. But my tame ladylove told me that when he went through the palace gates and saw the guardsmen in silver, and on the staircase the footmen in gold, he wasn't at all taken aback. He nodded and he said to them:

'"It must be very tiresome to stand on the stairs. I'd rather go inside."

'**T**he halls were brilliantly lighted. Ministers of state and privy councillors were walking about barefooted, carrying golden trays in front of them. It was enough to make anyone feel solemn, and his boots creaked dreadfully, but he wasn't a bit afraid.'

'That certainly must have been Kay,' said Gerda. 'I know he was wearing new boots. I heard them creaking in Grandmother's room.'

'Oh, they creaked all right,' said the crow. 'But it was little enough he cared as he walked straight to the Princess, who was sitting on a pearl as big as a spinning wheel. All the ladies-in-waiting with their attendants and their attendants' attendants, and all the lords-in-waiting with their gentlemen and their gentlemen's men, each of whom had his page with him, were standing there, and the nearer they stood to the door the more arrogant they looked. The gentlemen's men's pages, who always wore slippers, were almost too arrogant to look as they stood at the threshold.'

'That must have been terrible!' little Gerda exclaimed. 'And yet Kay won the Princess?'

'If I weren't a crow, I would have married her myself, for all that I'm engaged to another. They say he spoke as well as I do when I speak my crow language. Or so my tame ladylove tells me.

He was dashing and handsome, and he was not there to court the Princess but to hear her wisdom. This he liked, and she liked him.'

'Of course it was Kay,' said Gerda. 'He was so clever that he could do mental arithmetic even with fractions. Oh, please take me to the palace.'

'That's easy enough to say,' said the crow, 'but how can we manage it? I'll talk it over with my tame ladylove, and she may be able to suggest something, but I must warn you that a little girl like you will never be admitted.'

'Oh, yes I shall,' said Gerda. 'When Kay hears about me, he will come out to fetch me at once.'

'Wait for me beside that stile,' the crow said. He wagged his head and off he flew.

Darkness had set in when he got back.

'Caw, caw!' he said. 'My ladylove sends you her best wishes, and here's a little loaf of bread for you. She found it in the kitchen, where they have all the bread they need, and you must be hungry.

'ou simply can't get into the palace with those bare feet. The guardsmen in silver and the footmen in gold would never permit it. But don't you cry. We'll find a way. My ladylove knows of a little back staircase that leads up to the bedroom, and she knows where they keep the key to it.'

Then they went into the garden and down the wide promenade where the leaves were falling one by one. When, one by one, the lights went out in the palace, the crow led little Gerda to the back door, which stood ajar.

Oh, how her heart did beat with fear and longing. It was just as if she were about to do something wrong, yet she only wanted to make sure that this really was little Kay. Yes, truly it must be Kay, she thought, as she recalled his sparkling eyes and his long hair. She remembered exactly how he looked when he used to smile at her as they sat under the roses at home. Wouldn't he be glad to see her! Wouldn't he be interested in hearing how far she had come to find him, and how sad they had all been when he didn't come home. She was so frightened, and yet so happy.

Now they were on the stairway. A little lamp was burning on a cupboard, and there stood the tame crow, cocking her head to look at Gerda, who made the curtsy that her grandmother had taught her.

'My fiancé has told me many charming things about you, dear young lady,' she said. 'Your biography, as one might say, is very touching. Kindly take the lamp and I shall lead the way. We shall keep straight ahead, where we aren't apt to run into anyone.'

'It seems to me that someone is on the stairs behind us,' said Gerda. Things brushed past, and from the shadows on the wall they seemed to be horses with spindly legs and waving manes. And there were shadows of huntsmen, ladies and gentlemen, on horseback.

'Those are only dreams,' said the crow. 'They come to take the thoughts of their royal masters off to the chase. That's just as well, for it will give you a good opportunity to see them while they sleep. But I trust that, when you rise to high position and power, you will show a grateful heart.'

'Tut tut! You've no need to say that,' said the forest crow.

Now they entered the first room. It was hung with rose-coloured satin, embroidered with flowers.

he dream shadows were flitting by so fast that Gerda could not see the lords and ladies. Hall after magnificent hall quite bewildered her, until at last they reached the royal bedroom.

The ceiling of it was like the top of a huge palm tree, with leaves of glass, costly glass. In the middle of the room two beds hung from a massive stem of gold. Each of them looked like a lily. One bed was white, and there lay the Princess. The other was red, and there Gerda hoped to find little Kay. She bent one of the scarlet petals and saw the nape of a little brown neck. Surely this must be Kay. She called his name aloud and held the lamp near him. The dreams on horseback pranced into the room again, as he awoke – and turned his head – and it was not little Kay at all.

The Prince only resembled Kay about the neck, but he was young and handsome. The Princess peeked out of her lily-white bed, and asked what had happened. Little Gerda cried and told them all about herself, and about all that the crows had done for her.

'Poor little thing,' the Prince and the Princess said. They praised the crows, and said they weren't the least bit angry with them, but not to do it again. Furthermore, they should have a reward.

'Would you rather fly about without any responsibilities,' said the Princess, 'or would you care to be appointed court crows for life, with rights to all scraps from the kitchen?'

Both the crows bowed low and begged for permanent office, for they thought of their future and said it was better to provide for their 'old age,' as they called it.

The Prince got up, and let Gerda have his bed. It was the utmost that he could do.

She clasped her little hands and thought, 'How nice the people and the birds are.' She closed her eyes, fell peacefully asleep, and all the dreams came flying back again. They looked like angels, and they drew a little sled on which Kay sat. He nodded to her, but this was only in a dream, so it all disappeared when she woke up.

The next day she was dressed from her head to her heels in silk and in velvet too. They asked her to stay at the palace and have a nice time there, but instead she begged them to let her have a little carriage, a little horse, and a pair of little boots, so that she could drive out into the wide world to find Kay.

They gave her a pair of boots, and also a muff. They dressed her as nicely as could be and, when she was ready to go, there at the gate stood a brand-new carriage of pure gold. On it the coat of arms of the Prince and the Princess glistened like a star.

he coachman, the footman, and the postilions – four postilions there were – all wore golden crowns. The Prince and the Princess themselves helped her into the carriage, and wished her Godspeed. The forest crow, who was now a married man, accompanied her for the first three miles, and sat beside Gerda, for it upset him to ride backward. The other crow stood beside the gate and waved her wings. She did not accompany them because she was suffering from a headache, brought on by eating too much in her new position. Inside, the carriage was lined with sugared cookies, and the seats were filled with fruit and gingerbread.

'Fare you well, fare you well,' called the Prince and Princess. Little Gerda cried and the crow cried too, for the first few miles. Then the crow said goodbye, and that was the saddest leave-taking of all. He flew up into a tree and waved his big black wings as long as he could see the carriage, which flashed as brightly as the sun.

FIFTH STORY

THE LITTLE ROBBER GIRL

The carriage rolled on into a dark forest. Like a blazing torch, it shone in the eyes of some robbers. They could not bear it.

'That's gold! That's gold!' they cried. They sprang forward, seized the horses, killed the little postilions, the coachman, and the footman, and dragged little Gerda out of the carriage.

'How plump and how tender she looks, just as if she'd been fattened on nuts!' cried the old robber woman, who had a long bristly beard, and long eyebrows that hung down over her eyes. 'She looks like a fat little lamb. What a dainty dish she will be!' As she said this she drew out her knife, a dreadful, flashing thing.

'Ouch!' the old woman howled. At just that moment her own little daughter had bitten her ear. The little girl, whom she carried on her back, was a wild and reckless creature. 'You beasty brat!' her mother exclaimed, but it kept her from using that knife on Gerda.

'She shall play with me,' said the little robber girl. 'She must give me her muff and that pretty dress she wears, and sleep with me in my bed.'

And she again gave her mother such a bite that
the woman hopped and whirled around in pain. All
the robbers laughed, and shouted:

'See how she dances with her brat.'

'I want to ride in the carriage,' the little robber
girl said, and ride she did, for she was too spoiled
and headstrong for words. She and Gerda climbed
into the carriage and away they drove over stumps
and stones, into the depths of the forest. The little
robber girl was no taller than Gerda, but she was
stronger and much broader in the shoulders. Her
skin was brown and her eyes coal-black – almost sad
in their expression. She put her arms around Gerda,
and said:

'They shan't kill you unless I get angry with you.
I think you must be a princess.'

'No, I'm not,' said little Gerda. And she told
about all that had happened to her, and how much
she cared for little Kay. The robber girl looked at her
gravely, gave a little nod of approval and told her:

'Even if I should get angry with you, they shan't
kill you, because I'll do it myself!' Then she dried
Gerda's eyes, and stuck her own hands into Gerda's
soft, warm muff.

he carriage stopped at last, in the courtyard of a robber's castle. The walls of it were cracked from bottom to top. Crows and ravens flew out of every loophole, and bulldogs huge enough to devour a man jumped high in the air. But they did not bark, for that was forbidden.

In the middle of the stone-paved, smoky old hall, a big fire was burning. The smoke of it drifted up to the ceiling, where it had to find its own way out. Soup was boiling in a big cauldron, and hares and rabbits were roasting on the spit.

'Tonight you shall sleep with me and all my little animals,' the robber girl said. After they had something to eat and drink, they went over to a corner that was strewn with rugs and straw. On sticks and perches around the bedding roosted nearly a hundred pigeons. They seemed to be asleep, but they stirred just a little when the two little girls came near them.

'They are all mine,' said the little robber girl. She seized the one that was nearest to her, held it by the legs and shook it until it flapped its wings. 'Kiss it,' she cried, and thrust the bird in Gerda's face.

'hose two are the wild rascals,' she said, pointing high up the wall to a hole barred with wooden sticks. 'Rascals of the woods they are, and they would fly away in a minute if they were not locked up.

'And here is my old sweetheart, Bae,' she said, pulling at the antlers of a reindeer that was tethered by a shiny copper ring around his neck. 'We have to keep a sharp eye on him, or he would run away from us too. Every single night I tickle his neck with my knife blade, for he is afraid of that.' From a hole in the wall she pulled a long knife, and rubbed it against the reindeer's neck. After the poor animal had kicked up its heels, the robber girl laughed and pulled Gerda down into the bed with her.

'Are you going to keep that knife in bed with you?' Gerda asked, and looked at it a little frightened.

'I always sleep with my knife,' the little robber girl said. 'You never can tell what may happen. But let's hear again what you told me before about little Kay, and about why you are wandering through the wide world.'

Gerda told the story all over again, while the wild pigeons cooed in their cage overhead, and the tame pigeons slept. The little robber girl clasped one arm around Gerda's neck, gripped her knife in the other hand, fell asleep, and snored so that one could hear her. But Gerda could not close her eyes at all. She did not know whether she was to live or whether she was to die. The robbers sat around their fire, singing and drinking, and the old robber woman was turning somersaults. It was a terrible sight for a little girl to see.

Then the wood pigeons said, 'Coo, coo. We have seen little Kay. A white hen was carrying his sled, and Kay sat in the Snow Queen's sleigh. They swooped low, over the trees where we lay in our nest. The Snow Queen blew upon us, and all the young pigeons died except us. Coo, coo.'

'What is that you are saying up there?' cried Gerda. 'Where was the Snow Queen going? Do you know anything about it?'

'She was probably bound for Lapland, where they always have snow and ice. Why don't you ask the reindeer who is tethered beside you?'

'**Y**es, there is ice and snow in that glorious land,' the reindeer told her. 'You can prance about freely across those great, glittering fields. The Snow Queen has her summer tent there, but her stronghold is a castle up nearer the North Pole, on the island called Spitzbergen.'

'Oh, Kay, little Kay,' Gerda sighed.

'Lie still,' said the robber girl, 'or I'll stick my knife in your stomach.'

In the morning Gerda told her all that the wood pigeons had said. The little robber girl looked quite thoughtful. She nodded her head, and exclaimed, 'Leave it to me! Leave it to me.

'Do you know where Lapland is?' she asked the reindeer.

'Who knows it better than I?' the reindeer said, and his eyes sparkled. 'There I was born, there I was bred, and there I kicked my heels in freedom, across the fields of snow.'

'Listen!' the robber girl said to Gerda. 'As you see, all the men are away. Mother is still here, and here she'll stay, but before the morning is over she will drink out of that big bottle, and then she usually dozes off for a nap. As soon as that happens, I will do you a good turn.'

She jumped out of bed, rushed over and threw her arms around her mother's neck, pulled at her beard bristles, and said, 'Good morning, my dear nanny-goat.' Her mother thumped her nose until it was red and blue, but it was done out of pure love.

As soon as the mother had tipped up the bottle and dozed off to sleep, the little robber girl ran to the reindeer and said, 'I have a good notion to keep you here, and tickle you with my sharp knife. You are so funny when I do, but never mind that. I'll untie your rope, and help you find your way outside, so that you can run back to Lapland. But you must put your best leg forward and carry this little girl to the Snow Queen's palace, where her playmate is. I suppose you heard what she told me, for she spoke so loud, and you were eavesdropping.'

The reindeer was so happy that he bounded into the air. The robber girl hoisted little Gerda on his back, carefully tied her in place, and even gave her a little pillow to sit on. I don't do things halfway,' she said. 'Here, take back your fur boots, for it's going to be bitter cold. I'll keep your muff, because it's such a pretty one. But your fingers mustn't get cold. Here are my mother's big mittens, which will come right up to your elbows. Pull them on. Now your hands look just like my ugly mother's big paws.'

And Gerda shed happy tears.

'I don't care to see you blubbering,' said the little robber girl. 'You ought to look pleased now. Here, take these two loaves of bread and this ham along, so that you won't starve.'

When these provisions were tied on the back of the reindeer, the little robber girl opened the door and called in all the big dogs. Then she cut the tether with her knife and said to the reindeer, 'Now run, but see that you take good care of the little girl.'

Gerda waved her big mittens to the little robber girl, and said goodbye. Then the reindeer bounded away, over stumps and stones, straight through the great forest, over swamps and across the plains, as fast as he could run. The wolves howled, the ravens shrieked, and *ker-shew, ker-shew!* – the red streaks of light ripped through the heavens, with a noise that sounded like sneezing.

'Those are my old Northern Lights,' said the reindeer. 'See how they flash.' And on he ran, faster than ever, by night and day. The loaves were eaten and the whole ham was eaten – and there they were in Lapland.

SIXTH STORY
THE LAPP WOMAN AND
THE FINN WOMAN

They stopped in front of a little hut, and a make-shift dwelling it was. The roof of it almost touched the ground, and the doorway was so low that the family had to lie on their stomachs to crawl in to it or out of it. No one was at home except an old Lapp woman, who was cooking fish over a whale-oil lamp. The reindeer told her Gerda's whole story, but first he told his own, which he thought was much more important. Besides, Gerda was so cold that she couldn't say a thing.

'Oh, you poor creatures,' the Lapp woman said, 'you've still got such a long way to go. Why, you will have to travel hundreds of miles into the Finmark. For it's there that the Snow Queen is taking a country vacation, and burning her blue fireworks every evening. I'll jot down a message on a dried codfish, for I haven't any paper. I want you to take it to the Finn woman who lives up there. She will be able to tell you more about it than I can.'

As soon as Gerda had thawed out, and had had something to eat and drink, the Lapp woman wrote a few words on a dried codfish, told Gerda to take good care of it, and tied her again on the back of the reindeer. Off he ran, and all night long the skies crackled and swished as the most beautiful Northern Lights flashed over their heads. At last they came to the Finmark, and knocked at the Finn woman's chimney, for she hadn't a sign of a door.

It was so hot inside that the Finn woman went about almost naked. She was small and terribly dowdy, but she at once helped little Gerda off with her mittens and boots, and loosened her clothes. Otherwise the heat would have wilted her. Then the woman put a piece of ice on the reindeer's head, and read what was written on the codfish. She read it three times and when she knew it by heart, she put the fish into the kettle of soup, for they might as well eat it. She never wasted anything.

The reindeer told her his own story first, and then little Gerda's. The Finn woman winked a knowing eye, but she didn't say anything.

'You are such a wise woman,' said the reindeer, 'I know that you can tie all the winds of the world together with a bit of cotton thread. If the sailor unties one knot he gets a favourable wind. If he unties another he gets a stiff gale, while if he unties the third and fourth knots such a tempest rages that it flattens the trees in the forest. Won't you give this little girl something to drink that will make her as strong as twelve men, so that she may overpower the Snow Queen?'

'Twelve strong men,' the Finn woman sniffed. 'Much good that would be.'

She went to the shelf, took down a big rolled-up skin, and unrolled it. On this skin strange characters were written, and the Finn woman read them until the sweat rolled down her forehead.

ut the reindeer again begged her to help Gerda, and little Gerda looked at her with such tearful, imploring eyes that the woman began winking again. She took the reindeer aside in a corner, and while she was putting another piece of ice on his head she whispered to him:

'Little Kay is indeed with the Snow Queen, and everything there just suits him fine. He thinks it is the best place in all the world, but that's because he has a splinter of glass in his heart and a small piece of it in his eye. Unless these can be gotten out, he will never be human again, and the Snow Queen will hold him in her power.'

'But can't you fix little Gerda something to drink which will give her more power than all those things?'

'No power that I could give could be as great as that which she already has. Don't you see how men and beasts are compelled to serve her, and how far she has come in the wide world since she started out in her naked feet? We mustn't tell her about this power. Strength lies in her heart, because she is such a sweet, innocent child. If she herself cannot reach the Snow Queen and rid little Kay of those pieces of glass, then there's no help that we can give her.

The Snow Queen's garden lies about eight miles from here. You may carry the little girl there, and put her down by the big bush covered with red berries that grows on the snow. Then don't you stand there gossiping, but hurry to get back here.'

The Finn woman lifted little Gerda onto the reindeer, and he galloped away as fast as he could.

'Oh!' cried Gerda. 'I forgot my boots and I forgot my mittens.' She soon felt the need of them in that knife-like cold, but the reindeer did not dare to stop. He galloped on until they came to the big bush that was covered with red berries. Here he set Gerda down and kissed her on the mouth, while big shining tears ran down his face. Then he ran back as fast as he could. Little Gerda stood there without boots and without mittens, right in the middle of icy Finmark.

She ran as fast as ever she could. A whole regiment of snowflakes swirled towards her, but they did not fall from the sky, for there was not a cloud up there, and the Northern Lights were ablaze.

The flakes skirmished along the ground, and the nearer they came the larger they grew. Gerda remembered how large and strange they had appeared when she looked at them under the magnifying glass. But here they were much more monstrous and terrifying. They were alive.

hey were the Snow Queen's advance guard, and their shapes were most strange. Some looked like ugly, overgrown porcupines. Some were like a knot of snakes that stuck out their heads in every direction, and others were like fat little bears with every hair a-bristle. All of them were glistening white, for all were living snowflakes.

It was so cold that, as little Gerda said the Lord's Prayer, she could see her breath freezing in front of her mouth, like a cloud of smoke. It grew thicker and thicker, and took the shape of little angels that grew bigger and bigger the moment they touched the ground. All of them had helmets on their heads and they carried shields and lances in their hands. Rank upon rank, they increased, and when Gerda had finished her prayer she was surrounded by a legion of angels. They struck the dread snowflakes with their lances and shivered them into a thousand pieces. Little Gerda walked on, unmolested and cheerful. The angels rubbed her hands and feet to make them warmer, and she trotted briskly along to the Snow Queen's palace.

But now let us see how little Kay was getting on. Little Gerda was farthest from his mind, and he hadn't the slightest idea that she was just outside the palace.

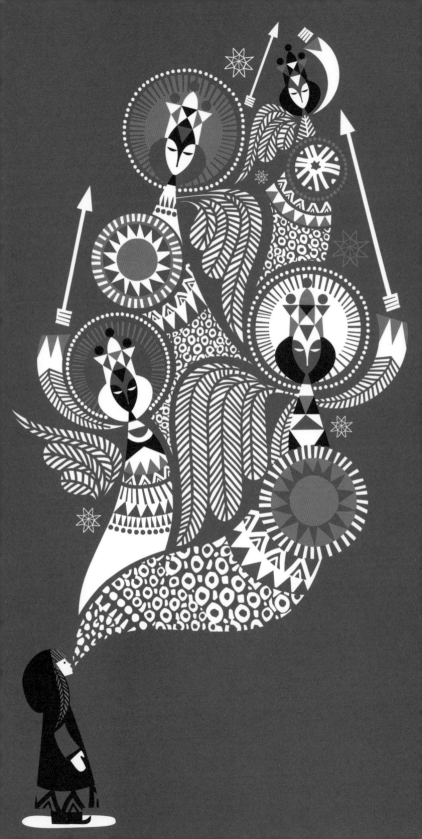

SEVENTH STORY

WHAT HAPPENED IN
THE SNOW QUEEN'S PALACE
AND WHAT CAME OF IT

The walls of the palace were driven snow. The windows and doors were the knife-edged wind. There were more than a hundred halls, shaped as the snow had drifted, and the largest of these extended for many a mile. All were lighted by the flare of the Northern Lights. All of the halls were so immense and so empty, so brilliant and so glacial! There was never a touch of gaiety in them; never so much as a little dance for the polar bears, at which the storm blast could have served for music, and the polar bears could have waddled about on their hind legs to show off their best manners. There was never a little party with such games as blind-bear's buff or hide the paw-kerchief for the cubs, nor even a little afternoon coffee over which the white fox vixens could gossip. Empty, vast, and frigid were the Snow Queen's halls. The Northern Lights flared with such regularity that you could time exactly when they would be at the highest and lowest. In the middle of the vast, empty hall of snow was a frozen lake. It was cracked into a thousand pieces, but each piece was shaped so exactly like the others that it seemed a work of wonderful craftsmanship. The Snow Queen sat in the exact centre of it when she was at home, and she spoke of this as sitting on her 'Mirror of Reason.' She said this mirror was the only one of its kind, and the best thing in all the world.

Little Kay was blue, yes, almost black, with the cold. But he did not feel it, because the Snow Queen had kissed away his icy tremblings, and his heart itself had almost turned to ice.

He was shifting some sharp, flat pieces of ice to and fro, trying to fit them into every possible pattern, for he wanted to make something with them. It was like the Chinese puzzle game that we play at home, juggling little flat pieces of wood about into special designs. Kay was cleverly arranging his pieces in the game of ice-cold reason. To him the patterns were highly remarkable and of the utmost importance, for the chip of glass in his eye made him see them that way. He arranged his pieces to spell out many words; but he could never find the way to make the one word he was so eager to form. The word was 'Eternity.' The Snow Queen had said to him, 'If you can puzzle that out you shall be your own master, and I'll give you the whole world and a new pair of skates.' But he could not puzzle it out.

'Now I am going to make a flying trip to the warm countries,' the Snow Queen told him. 'I want to go and take a look into the black cauldrons.' She meant the volcanoes of Etna and Vesuvius. 'I must whiten them up a bit. They need it, and it will be such a relief after all those yellow lemons and purple grapes.'

And away she flew. Kay sat all alone in that endless, empty, frigid hall, and puzzled over the pieces of ice until he almost cracked his skull. He sat so stiff and still that one might have thought he was frozen to death.

All of a sudden, little Gerda walked up to the palace through the great gate, which was a knife-edged wind. But Gerda said her evening prayer. The wind was lulled to rest, and the little girl came on into the vast, cold, empty hall. Then she saw Kay. She recognised him at once, and ran to throw her arms around him. She held him close and cried, 'Kay, dearest little Kay! I've found you at last!'

But he sat still, and stiff, and cold. Gerda shed hot tears, and when they fell upon him they went straight to his heart. They melted the lump of ice and burned away the splinter of glass in it. He looked up at her, and she sang:

'Where roses bloom so sweetly in the vale,
There shall you find the Christ Child, without fail.'

Kay burst into tears. He cried so freely that the little piece of glass in his eye was washed right out. 'Gerda!' He knew her, and cried out in his happiness, 'My sweet little Gerda, where have you been so long? And where have I been?'

e looked around him and said, 'How cold it is here! How enormous and empty!' He held fast to Gerda, who laughed until happy tears rolled down her cheeks. Their bliss was so heavenly that even the bits of ice danced about them and shared in their happiness. When the pieces grew tired, they dropped into a pattern which made the very word that the Snow Queen had told Kay he must find before he became his own master and received the whole world and a new pair of skates.

Gerda kissed his cheeks, and they turned pink again. She kissed his eyes, and they sparkled like hers. She kissed his hands and feet, and he became strong and well. The Snow Queen might come home now whenever she pleased, for there stood the order for Kay's release, written in letters of shining ice.

Hand in hand, Kay and Gerda strolled out of that enormous palace. They talked about Grandmother, and about the roses on their roof. Wherever they went, the wind died down and the sun shone out. When they came to the bush that was covered with red berries, the reindeer was waiting to meet them. He had brought along a young reindeer mate who had warm milk for the children to drink, and who kissed them on the mouth.

Then these reindeer carried Gerda and Kay first to the Finn woman. They warmed themselves in her hot room, and when she had given them directions for their journey home they rode on to the Lapp woman. She had made them new clothes, and was ready to take them along in her sleigh.

Side by side, the reindeer ran with them to the limits of the North country, where the first green buds were to be seen. Here they said goodbye to the two reindeer and to the Lapp woman. 'Farewell,' they all said.

Now the first little birds began to chirp, and there were green buds all around them in the forest. Through the woods came riding a young girl on a magnificent horse that Gerda recognised, for it had once been harnessed to the golden carriage. The girl wore a bright red cap on her head, and a pair of pistols in her belt. She was the little robber girl, who had grown tired of staying at home, and who was setting out on a journey to the North country. If she didn't like it there, why, the world was wide, and there were many other places where she could go. She recognised Gerda at once, and Gerda knew her too. It was a happy meeting.

'ou're a fine one for gadding about,' she told little Kay. 'I'd just like to know whether you deserve to have someone running to the end of the earth for your sake.'

But Gerda patted her cheek and asked her about the Prince and the Princess.

'They are travelling in foreign lands,' the robber girl told her.

'And the crow?'

'Oh, the crow is dead,' she answered. 'His tame ladylove is now a widow, and she wears a bit of black wool wrapped around her leg. She takes great pity on herself, but that's all stuff and nonsense. Now tell me what has happened to you and how you caught up with Kay.'

Gerda and Kay told her their story.

'*Snip snap snurre, basse lurre,*' said the robber girl. 'So everything came out all right.' She shook them by the hand, and promised that if ever she passed through their town she would come to see them. And then she rode away.

Kay and Gerda held each other by the hand. And as they walked along they had wonderful spring weather. The land was green and strewn with flowers, church bells rang, and they saw the high steeples of a big town.

It was the one where they used to live. They walked straight to Grandmother's house, and up the stairs, and into the room, where everything was just as it was when they left it. And the clock said *tick-tock*, and its hands were telling the time. But the moment they came in the door they noticed one change. They were grown-up now.

The roses on the roof looked in at the open window, and their two little stools were still out there. Kay and Gerda sat down on them, and held each other by the hand. Both of them had forgotten the icy, empty splendour of the Snow Queen's palace as completely as if it were some bad dream. Grandmother sat in God's good sunshine, reading to them from her Bible:

'Except ye become as little children, ye shall not enter into the Kingdom of Heaven.'

Kay and Gerda looked into each other's eyes, and at last they understood the meaning of their old hymn:

'Where roses bloom so sweetly in the vale,
There shall you find the Christ Child, without fail.'

And they sat there, grown up, but children still – children at heart. And it was summer, warm, glorious summer.

The End

HANS CHRISTIAN ANDERSEN was born in Odense, Denmark, in 1805. The son of a cobbler and a washerwoman, he didn't start school until he was seventeen. He became famous for his fairy tales, including classics such as *The Ugly Duckling* and *The Little Mermaid*. *The Snow Queen* was published in 1844. When he died aged 70, the king and crown prince of Denmark attended his funeral.

SANNA ANNUKKA spent her childhood summers in Finland, and its landscape and folklore remain a source of inspiration. A print maker and illustrator based in Brighton, England, she is also a designer for Finnish textile brand Marimekko and has been featured in *Vogue* and many interior design magazines. She has also illustrated Hans Christian Andersen's *The Fir Tree*.